Illustrations c 1967 Patmos-Verlag, Dusseldorf
English Text c 1969 Macdonald & Co. (Publishers) Ltd.
First published in the United States of America in 1969 by Scroll Press, Inc., 22 E. 84th St.,
New York, N.Y. 10028
First published in Great Britain in 1970 by Macdonald & Co. (Publishers) Ltd.,
49 Poland Street, London W.1.
Library of Congress No 71-106506.
Printed in Germany
SBN 356 031918

They Followed
the Star

Štěpán Zavřel

Scroll Press Inc.

Night falls on the land,
deep, dark night,
and everyone is asleep.

Asleep in the hills . . .

Asleep in the great cities . . .

Asleep in the castles . . .

. . . and asleep in the cottages.

All is still, and no one knows
what the night will bring.

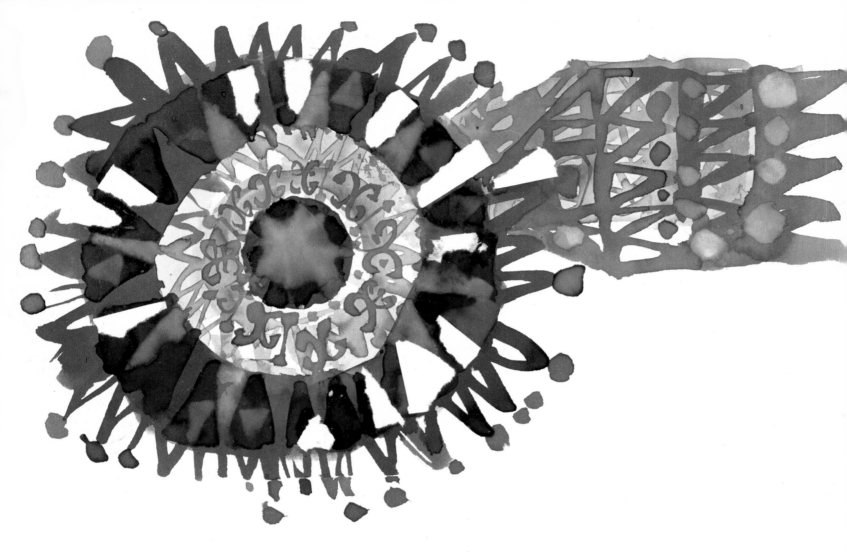

Yet this is a night like no other.

For on this night
a new star suddenly shines in the sky.

It is larger and brighter
and more beautiful than all the other stars.
On the hillside shepherds awake and stare around them.
The sky is bright, and they hear angels singing
and playing heavenly music.

The angels tell them,
"Tonight, Christ, the promised Messiah, is born."

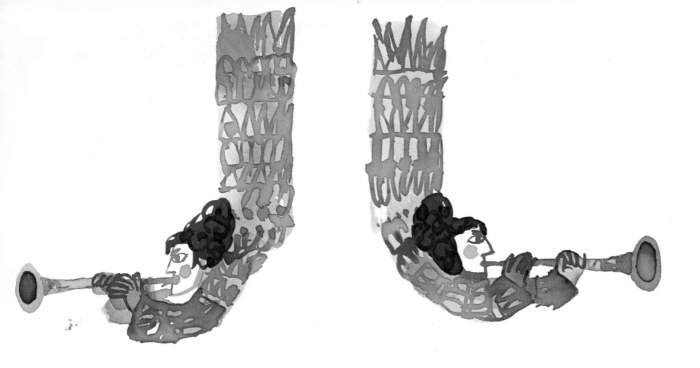

On this night, so dark and so still,
on this night when the beautiful star shines in the heavens,
three wise men lie sleeping far away in the East—three great kings.
They sleep . . .
But the star moves across the sky until it rests
over each of the palaces where the kings lie.
Suddenly, all the land is bright with light,
and the first and then the second of the wise men
awakes to hear the message
the angels bring.

This is the long awaited day.
They read over the old prophecies
about the Messiah, and they rejoice.
Then the first two kings set off
on their journey.

The third king is still sleeping in his splendid palace.
But the star comes.
"Arise, the Messiah is born," calls the angel from the heavens.
And so the third king prepares for the journey
and joins the other two.
The three kings know they have very far to travel.
Although they have never met before,
they are all following the star for the same reason —
it will lead them to Christ, the King of Kings.
They have gifts for him,
gold and frankincense and myrrh.

The star moves on ahead of them.

Ever westward they travel
passing through villages and towns
journeying night and day on and on . . .
Then one morning they come to the edge of a great desert.
The desert is dry, hot and bare.
But the star moves out over the desert, and they follow
without fear across the rolling sands.
They know they must follow the star.

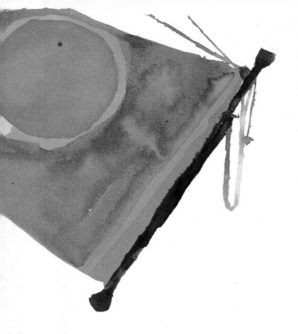

They pass through many villages.
They climb over many mountain passes.
And finally they reach the sea.
It stretches away from them
to the distant horizon—endlessly.
Only a single ship lies at anchor by the shore.

They find that the coins they have brought with them
are not enough to pay for their passage.
It seems they can go no farther.
But they know the newborn King is waiting for them,
and they must not delay.

As they have nothing else with them,
they give the captain their crowns.
Now they have paid for their passage,
they can continue their journey.

High up on the ship's mast
they gaze at the arching skies
and greet the other ships that pass them.
They see many islands
and the towering cliffs
of distant lands.
And still they travel on . . .

After many days at sea,
their ship reaches port.
The wise men set off again
following their star.
At last they reach a great city,
golden and gleaming
and filled with splendid buildings.

It is a mysterious city
surrounded by a high wall
with towers that reach up to the sky.
The wise men have never seen
such a city before.
The city is called
"Jerusalem the Golden."

They enter by a gate
under a high arch
and make their way past gardens
and wells of clear water
until they arrive
in front of a huge palace.
It is the palace of King Herod!

Herod talks with the wise men
and asks them where they are going
and who this king is that they seek.
His voice is smooth and kind,
but his heart is full of jealous anger.
He does not think his throne will be safe
if another king is alive in his country.
So Herod decides to kill this newborn King.
He does not understand the prophecies about the Messiah
who is to save mankind.
He allows the three wise men to continue on their journey
but orders them to tell him on their way back
where he can find the newborn King.

The wise men depart.
Herod laughs,
saying to his courtiers,
"Sharpen your swords;
you are going to need them."
And his courtiers laugh, too.

But as the three wise men
are leaving the city,
an angel warns them
what the wicked king
is planning.

The angel tells them not to visit Jerusalem on their way home.
So they travel on
until the star stops above a small town.

It is Bethlehem.

They wipe the dust from their sandals and polish
the golden caskets containing their gifts until the gold shines.
They mop their brows and straighten
and tidy their robes.

Then they come to where the shepherds are worshipping
the Christ Child. Bowing low before Him, they give Him their gifts,
gold and frankincense and myrrh.
They hail Him "King of kings."

When the shepherds see
these great kings bow down to the Child
they understand
that He is not only to reign over simple men like themselves
but also over the wisest and most powerful of kings.
They realize
that the Messiah has come to save all men,
the rich who live in palaces
and the poor who sleep out under the stars.